Based on the TV series *Rugrats*® created by Arlene Klasky, Gabor Csupo, and Paul Germain as seen on NICKELODEON®

SIMON SPOTLIGHT
An imprint of Simon & Schuster
Children's Publishing Division
1230 Avenue of the Americas
New York, NY 10020

This edition published by Grolier Books.
Grolier Books is a division of Grolier Enterprises, Inc.

ISBN 0-7172-8989-3

Major-League DADS

By Molly Wigand
Illustrated by Vince Giarrano

Ready-to-Read

Simon Spotlight/Nickelodeon

Tommy, Chuckie, Angelica, Phil, and Lil walked up the big steps with their dads and Grandpa Lou.

"Welcome to Slugger Stadium!" said a loud voice. "And Happy Father's Day to all you dads out there!"

"Yes," said Chas. "Happy Father's Day to us!"

The loud voice added, "Today, some lucky dads will play ball with the pros!"

"How do you play ball with crows?" Chuckie asked.

"Here are our seats," said Stu.

The crowd began to sing. Angelica sang, too.

"For the land of the fleas, and the home of the brain!" she yelled.

"Play ball!" cried Grandpa Lou.

"Watch the game, kids!" said Stu.

"Forget the game!" said Angelica. She pointed to a man carrying a cooler. "Watch *him!*"

"Ice cream! Get your ice cream!" the man yelled.

"Gimme ice cream!" shouted Angelica.

Chas bought ice
cream for everyone.
The ice cream was
good—good
and messy!

A woman walked by. She had a big tray.
"Look—pink clouds!" said Phil.
"On a stick!" said Lil.
"Cotton candy! Get your cotton candy!"
the woman said.

"Gimme cotton candy!" yelled
Angelica.
  "Five cotton candies," said Stu.
The cotton candy was good
and sticky!

"Batter up!" said the umpire.

"That batter has a nice swing," Drew said.

"Did you hear that?" Tommy asked the babies.

"Maybe he has a merry-go-round, too!" said Phil.

"And monkey bars!" said Lil.

"Let's go find them!" Tommy said.

"Uh, do we have to?" asked Chuckie.

"Foul ball!" yelled the umpire.
The ball flew toward the dads!

"I got it!" yelled Chas.

"I got it!" yelled Stu.

"I got it!" yelled Howard.

"No, I got it!" yelled Drew.

"Outta my way!" yelled Grandpa Lou.

"We all got it!" said the men.

"High fives!"

"Here's our chance," said Tommy. "Let's go to the swings!"

"Are you coming, Angelica?" Lil asked.

"Hah!" said Angelica. "Swings are for babies. I'm gonna find more cotton candy."

"These are big stairs," said Phil.

"And there are so many," Lil added.

"Come on babies, do it the fast way—
ride down on your bottoms!" said Tommy.

They bumped down the stairs.

"Thank Bob for diapies," said Phil.

At the bottom of the stairs, they saw a man with a bat.

"I don't see any swings," said Chuckie.

"And I don't see any cotton candy!" said Angelica. "This has been a wild moose chase!"

Just then, another man stood up. "Look!" he shouted. "That runner is stealing home!"

"Did you hear that?" asked Phil. "That man is stealing home!"

"Then where will we sleep?" asked Chuckie.

"Who will take care of Spike?" asked Tommy. "And Dil?"

"And Cynthia!" yelled Angelica.

"Come on, guys!" said Tommy. "We've got to stop him!"

The dads watched the game.
"Hey, maybe we should get hot dogs for the kids," said Stu.

"Wait—where are the kids?" asked Chas.
The men looked around. Then they
spotted a pink trail on the stairs.
"Follow that goo!" yelled Grandpa Lou.

"Help!" cried Angelica. "Some mean guy stole my home!"

The babies began to cry.

The dads found the babies by the dugout. Angelica sniffed, "That man stole our home!" Drew smiled. "It's okay, kids," he said. "He just ran to *home plate*! *Our* home is safe and sound."

A baseball player went over to the dads.

"Are you guys in the contest?" he asked. "Follow me, it's almost time!"

The dads were excited. They were going to play ball with the pros!

Music began to play.

"Hey, it's the seventh-inning scratch," said Angelica.

"Take me out to the ball game, shake me out with the clowns!" she sang.

The dads and Grandpa Lou ran onto the field.

"These lucky dads will try to catch the ball," said the announcer. "Batter up!"

First, Howard and Drew each caught a ball. Everyone clapped.

Then Stu and Chas each caught a ball. Everyone cheered.

When it was Grandpa Lou's turn, he dove for the ball. Then he fell down. But he rolled over—and caught the ball!

The crowd roared.

"Good job," said the baseball player. "Please sit with us for the rest of the game."

"Whoo-hoo!" yelled all the dads.

"What a great Father's Day!" Stu said.
"Cotton candy for everyone!" called Grandpa Lou.
"About time," said Angelica.

Rugrats™

YUKS
-n-
STUFF

Tommy in Charge

Whenever there's a problem, Tommy knows what to do. I remember the time

- He took us on an "expulition" to the North Pole to see Santa Claus.

- We went into Grandpa Lou's room to face the big bed monster.

- He found a way to get out of the day care center.

- He took us to find the flusher to flush the giant potty (the grown-ups called it "the swimming pool").

- He told Angelica that we weren't going to make any more lemonade until she started sharing all the dimes.

- Tommy became Changing Boy to save the Mega-Hyper Heroes from Angelica.

- We went all over the place to find a moose.

- Tommy even went into the next yard, where the scary big dog lives, so he could get his ball back.

When They Grow Up

Someday all the babies will grow up. What will they become?

TOMMY

- An explorer
- A cowboy
- Or even the President!

CHUCKIE

- A safety inspector
- A hairdresser
- Or just like his dad

PHIL

- A taste-tester
- A bug collector
- Or the manager of the Minnesota Twins

LIL

- A bait shop owner
- A lawyer
- Or a hair bow manufacturer!

ANGELICA

- A prank shop owner
- A spoiled fruit inspector
- But probably a boss like mommy

Joke Break

What do dinosaurs put on their fish sandwiches?

Reptar sauce.

What did the belly button say just before it left.

"I'm outtie here!"

What do you get when you cross a bunny and a puppy?

A hop dog.

Who's every sheep's favorite superhero?

Baaaaatman.

What do you get if you cross
Tommy's dad with a cow?
Beef Stu.

Why did Reptar
get a ticket?
He ran through a
stomp sign.

Where
does Lil's
twin go
when he's
out of gas?
The Philling station.

What do baby
cats wear?
Diapurrs.

What Kind of Keys does
Tommy like to carry?
Cookies.

Grandpa Lou's Tall Tales

Tommy's grandpa likes to talk about the past. But sometimes his stories are a little hard to believe.

GRANDPA:

"When I was a sprout, if we wanted entertainment, we went out back and pulled up stumps."

TOMMY:

"Was that for your stump collection?"

GRANDPA:

"There we were, hunkered down in the shadow of an enormous bull moose, just a hair bigger than this house. The whole Pickles clan had moose for breakfast, lunch, and dinner the remainder of the Great Depression."

PHIL:

"I'd rather eat bugs than mooses."

GRANDPA:

"When I was a sprout, I used to crawl through Ma's cactus garden huntin' for horned toads. And all I had on was my birthday suit!"

LIL: "Ouch!"

GRANDPA:

"Reminds me of the fifteen years I spent prospectin' up in the Yukon. One night it got so cold I had to sleep under a grizzly bear."

ANGELICA:

"I can't BEAR any more of these stories!"